LOST BEHIND ENEMY LINES

LOST BEHIND ENEMY LINES

A Vietnam Veteran's True Story
of Survival and the Revelation of
Physical and Spiritual Warfare

DANNY CLIFFORD

Cover by: Lisa Hainline Award-Winning Graphic Designer of
LIONSGATE Book Design, *LionsgateBookDesign.com*

Edited by: **Frank W. Kresen**/*proof positive*, frankkresen@
hotmail.com
Interior Designed and Formatted by: **Steve Plummer,**
SPBookDesign.com

EDITORS REVIEW

ALMOST ALL OF us know someone who had been deployed to Vietnam. But most of the veterans don't want to talk about their Vietnam experiences. So, for me, this is the first realistic, packed-with-details account of what daily life was like in Vietnam that I've ever read.

You will enjoy *Lost Behind Enemy Lines: A Vietnam Veteran's True Story of Survival and the Revelation of Physical and Spiritual Warfare*, a firsthand description of the reality of being in the "infantry boots on the ground" of Danny Clifford, a US Army Ranger Team Leader in Vietnam, on a mission behind enemy lines.

Danny Clifford's account of despair turning to hope and ending in a miraculous rescue from a large enemy force in Vietnam will be seen as a parallel to what a Christian experiences when their life is changed and saved by an act of God.

In the second half of the book, Clifford paints an explicit picture of the parallels between Earthly military combat and the spiritual battle for their soul that human beings endure every single day of their lives.

It's not difficult to imagine Clifford's Ranger Team's extraction by helicopter, with the rescued soldiers hanging on to a rope ladder for dear life far, far above the ground, as the battlefield equivalent of The Rapture—not to mention the vision of Jacob's Ladder.

Editor
Frank W. Kresen

AUTHOR INTRODUCTION

Lost behind Enemy Lines is a true story of my experiences and training as a US Army Airborne Rangers performing reconnaissance missions in the central highlands of South Vietnam.

My book will captivate you and take you on a mission where you'll be *Lost Behind Enemy Lines*, and experience the reality of being in my infantry boots "on the ground" as a US Army Ranger Team Leader with no radio communication and ambushed by enemy trail watchers guarding a battalion base camp. You'll experience running from an enemy that far out-numbers you, until your exhausted and experience the emotion of utter hopelessness.

To survive in Vietnam and come home alive required elite mental and physical training and the discipline to perform our mission in extreme conditions. If we got distracted and disobeyed or ignored our training, our opportunity of survival was greatly diminished.

There was a lot of things to distract us in Vietnam such as drugs, alcohol, sex, pornography, and the thrill of living on the edge. These distractions were our un-seen spiritual enemies that we faced daily—ready to destroy us—before we even went on a mission to face our physical human enemies.

The second half of *Lost Behind Enemy Lines* compares the similarities of the tactics and principals used to survive the warfare in Vietnam—too to those needed to endure through the Spiritual warfare that occurs daily for the soul of every human being.

You'll truly enjoy it. I promise!

Author,
Danny Clifford

DEDICATION

I DEDICATE THIS BOOK to my beautiful wife, Michelle. You believed in what God was doing in me!

I am forever grateful to God for allowing you to enter my life at just the right moment and become my best friend, confidante, and lover. Without your encouragement, your smile, and your generosity, this book would never have been written.

You are even more beautiful on the inside than you are on the outside. I love you more than you'll ever know.

Thank you for being my caring friend and for loving me, even though at times it's not easy. J

ACKNOWLEDGEMENTS

Heather Clifford, my daughter, makes me beam with humble pride by the life she lives. I have never told her how great a teacher she is, but I should have, as I have learned a great deal from watching her and listening to her. She cares for other people more than she does for herself, always giving of herself until she hurts. She loves God and understands why He put her on earth. God has blessed her with a wonderful husband Ben, and so far a lovely son, Gabriel James. No he's no angel.

To my son Danny, when you were young I didn't teach you about God. He wasn't a priority in my life then. But

God never gave up on us. He found me 14 years ago and He found you two years ago. Continue to grow your relationship with God. Thank you for being my son and loving me while I learned to be a father. I love you dearly and am fortunate and pleased to have you as my son.

Thank you for your service to our country as a US Army airborne soldier. Today, Danny continues to serve America, performing security work throughput the world, as a civilian.

Bishop Steve Coleman, of Williams Temple Church of God in Christ in Portland, Maine, played an important role in my decision to begin a new life with Jesus Christ. If not for the Bishop's Early-Sunday-morning Bible studies, where would I be? Bishop Coleman is a strong yet humble teacher of the Word of God, whom I have come to love as my brother, my competitive fishing partner, and my Pastor who conducted our marriage. He loves God and is a compassionate leader for the sheep he leads. I enjoy his teaching and eating his sandwiches while fishing. Thank you for setting the example of excellence. In a time of war, we would call Bishop Coleman a *pathfinder.*

David Thete: I had just dedicated my life to Christ when, one Sunday morning, I was kneeling down at the altar, praying, and God put a young boy, six years old, beside me to pray. As I was praying, I was distracted by his prayer, so I stopped to listen. He was praying, with conviction, for other people, asking God to help this one and provide food and clothes for that one. As I listened, I broke down weeping. He was praying for others, not himself. David, his mother Adele, and two sisters, Dorcas and Marielle, are refugees from the Congo, in Africa, whom God introduced my wife and me to, so that we could learn what faith really was.

Through David, God taught me that I must come to God as a child. David is my adopted son and when he prays asking God to allow us to catch fish, David always gets more fish!

Pastor Adam Alexander, Tehilla Tabernacle Ministries, Westbrook, Maine, is a Pastor I respect, a brother, a mentor, and a friend from whom I have learned much by watching and observing him while on missions with him in Maine and in Texas with "Hurricane Ike." By being around Pastor Adam, I now know what it would have been like trying to keep up with the Apostle Paul. Pastor Adam taught me well.

To Jesus, the Only Begotten Son of God and recipient of the Medal of Honor; awarded to him for Saving the human race by sacrificing His life for us, in our place.

FOREWORD
BY MICHELLE CLIFFORD

FIRST, I WOULD like to thank God Almighty for the work, desire, passion, and anointing He has placed upon and within you. I've had the privilege not only of watching the Holy Spirit water the many seeds that have been planted inside your heart throughout your lifetime but also experiencing firsthand the unveiling of spiritual revelations regarding the Word as you've gone from a baby, drinking milk, to a man, digesting food of substance.

This is the beginning of many things God has appointed for your journey—called Life—as you start a process of sharing and releasing the Gospel to those who may not have heard or known the Truth.

Thank you for being my friend, my husband, my teacher, and my covering.

With love,

Michelle

"For this is good and acceptable in the sight of God our Savior, who desires all men to be saved and to come to the knowledge of the truth. For there is one God and one Mediator between God and men, the Man Christ Jesus, who gave Himself a ransom for all, to be testified in due time, for which I was appointed a preacher and an apostle—I am speaking the truth in Christ and not lying—a teacher of the Gentiles in faith and truth."

(I Timothy 2:3-7, *NKJV*)

CONTENTS

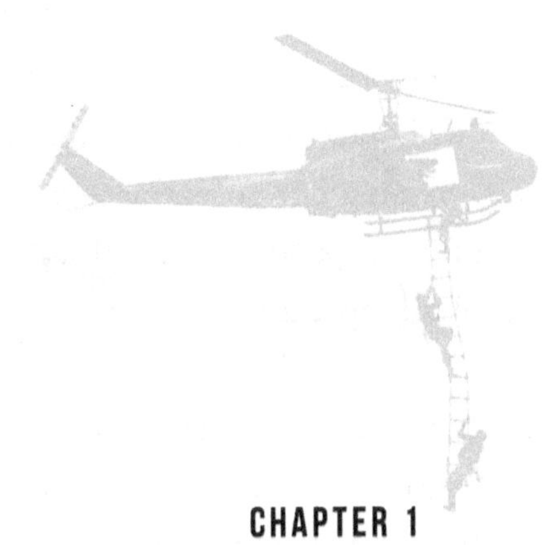

CHAPTER 1

A RANGER IN VIETNAM

BY THE END of 1967, the United States had been supporting an escalating war in South Vietnam for four years with little progress of winning or ending the war. Thousands of United States soldiers had been killed, and hundreds of thousands more had been wounded supporting South Vietnam's civil war for independence against North Vietnam's invading Regular Army and rebels from South Vietnam, called Viet Cong. North Vietnam was heavily supported by two Communist countries, China and Russia.

In 1967 and 1968, many citizens in the United States were protesting against the war in Vietnam. They wanted the government to withdraw and get out. Other citizens supported the war, wanting our government to stay and defeat communism from expanding in Southeast Asia by supporting and establishing a democratic government in South Vietnam.

This disagreement peaked and erupted into emotional and occasionally violent protest on hundreds of college campuses and in cities throughout the United States.

This was a serious and life-changing event for veterans who had spent a year away from family and loved ones and survived the horrors of Vietnam—only to return home and, instead of being welcomed and appreciated when they arrived, were spit on, ridiculed, and called names by some who opposed the war.

On January 31, 1968, an estimated 100,000 North Vietnamese and Viet Cong forces launched the Tet Offensive, a coordinated series of vicious attacks on more than 100 cities and towns in South Vietnam. During this Tet Offensive (named for the lunar new year holiday called Tet), the United States Embassy in South Vietnam's capital city of Saigon was overrun by a platoon of Viet Cong enemy soldiers. This attack stunned U.S. and international observers, who saw images of the carnage broadcast on television as it occurred.

North Vietnam achieved a strategic victory with the

1968 Tet Offensive, as the attacks marked a turning point in the Vietnam War and the beginning of the slow, painful American withdrawal from Southeast Asia.

During the 1960s, the United States Army drafted personnel to fill its needs. A young man coming out of high school had about a 90 percent chance of being drafted into the United States Army and forced to go to Vietnam. That was the setting in 1968, when I graduated from high school, so that, in the fall of 1968, I enlisted into the United States Army as an airborne infantryman and volunteered to go to Vietnam.

At basic training, the Army trained us in the same conventional warfare tactics that had been taught to the Armed Forces during World War II and the Korean War. That training consisted of conquering, occupying, and controlling territory by seizing the high ground around it. We were trained to operate and advance our positions by maneuvering in company-sized (about 150 soldiers) or battalion-sized forces (about 500-600 soldiers).

By the fall of 1969, the Vietnam War had killed and wounded so many Army non-commissioned officers that the US Army had started a five-month non-commissioned officers training school at Fort Benning, Georgia, to replenish and ensure that they had enough ranking squad and platoon leaders available to fight the war in Vietnam.

The school had two stages of infantry-leadership training: Phase one was three months in Fort Benning learning the tasks and responsibilities of an infantry E-5 sergeant and E-6 staff-sergeant. Phase two training was when we were promoted to E-5 and sent to an advanced infantry training center, where we became platoon sergeants training a platoon of soldiers who had just graduated basic training and who were now to be trained in advanced infantry skills.

I volunteered for the non-commissioned officers school and graduated Staff Sergeant E-6 in the early fall of 1969. After eleven months of training in the United States Army, I was fully trained and given overseas orders to report to the 173rd Airborne Division in Vietnam.

When I arrived in Vietnam for in-country processing, a team of Rangers were conducting recruiting meetings for volunteers to join the 75th Airborne Ranger Battalion. I went to their presentation and listened as they explained how the 75th Ranger Battalion assigned a company of Rangers to each United States Army division throughout Vietnam. A company of Rangers consisted of about 150 Rangers, operating twelve to fifteen six-man teams, plus support personnel.

They explained that the Ranger Team mission was to sneak around behind enemy lines and gather intelligence on the enemy and/or capture a prisoner of war (POW), if possible, and get out of the area undetected. The purpose of their missions was to provide up-to-date information on enemy activity to battalion and division intelligence staffs. A team's mission usually lasted for four days and three nights, covering an area of responsibility of about four to six square miles.

If a Ranger Team got into a fire-fight, their mission was considered compromised, and they needed to be extracted out of harm's way immediately. For that reason, Ranger Teams had priority in receiving fire-power, medical, and extraction support from the air, sea, and ground, over company- and battalion-sized units that may also be in a combat fire-fight with the enemy.

After each mission, a Ranger Team had three days to stand down and prepare for the next mission. There was also a rewards program which included three days off for capturing a POW alive and/or capturing important documents.

They bragged how good the food was: Dehydrated lightweight LRRP rations (Long Range Reconnaissance Patrol). Just add water, and you had your choice of the best chili with beans and rice, chicken and rice, beef stew, or chicken stew.

One of the most powerful-air support weapons at the Rangers' disposal was "Puff the Magic Dragon," a C-130 large cargo airplane with an ordnance of several mini-guns aboard. Each mini-gun was capable of firing 5,000 rounds per minute. That's placing a bullet in every square inch of a football field in a matter of 30 seconds, and every fourth round was a tracer. At night, it looked like a stream of fire coming from heaven to earth, with a continuous sound of a *Burrrrrrrup*! That's how it got the name "Puff the Magic Dragon"—the worst nightmare the enemy could have had. It was our secret weapon.

The Rangers conveyed to us four basic ways a Ranger Team's mission could end.

One way was, after spending four days and three nights of quietly maneuvering through their assigned area, the Ranger Team would be extracted at a predesignated landing zone at a prearranged time.

Another way for a mission to end was, after monitoring enemy movement on a trail, they would set an ambush, hoping to capture a POW or rucksacks with maps and information. Once the ambush happened, the Rangers' mission and location were considered compromised and they needed to be extracted immediately.

The most fearful ending to a Ranger Team's mission was being ambushed at night while sleeping in their night position. To avoid this, Ranger Teams walked past their selected night position and then made a half circle back to where they would rest for the evening. Picture a fish hook lying down, with the sharpest point of the fish-hook being the night location. This fish-hook maneuver allowed the Ranger Team to monitor and ambush the trail that led into their night position.

Once in their final night position, they set up trip flares along their trail to warn them of an enemy in pursuit of them. Then they positioned Claymore mines aimed at covering the entire trail that led to their location. They would frequently attach a trip flare to the Claymore mines as a booby trap, to ensure that the enemy didn't sneak in on them and turn the Claymore mines around on the Ranger team.

Claymore mines were one of the most devastating weapons in Vietnam. The Claymore mine used 1 1/2 pounds of C-4 explosive, shaped in an outward-curved block. It contained 700 1/8-inch-diameter steel balls placed in front of the C-4. A 100-foot roll of electronic wire connected the blasting cap in the Claymore to the electronic firing device in the Ranger's hand. When detonated, the Claymore's horrendous explosive force formed the relatively 700 soft steel balls into a shape similar to that of a 22 caliber bullet, with an effective casualty range of about 50 yards, resulting in about 30 percent of a man's body covered with wounds from the Claymore.

In order for the enemy to locate Rangers at night, they would follow their trail—but when they did, a well-prepared surprise awaited them. When a flare went up, Rangers were already in a prone position and could easily see the enemy. They would detonate their Claymore mines, and while the noise and falling debris settled, the Rangers quietly ran off to a pre-arranged night-extraction location. The rules of engagement at night were not to fire their rifle unless they absolutely had to, as the muzzle flash would give their location away.

The most dangerous ending for a Ranger Team's mission was being ambushed. In such a scenario, they gathered up any wounded Rangers and ran. As they ran, they communicated their situation and location, requested support from helicopter gun-ships, artillery, and Jet F-4 air-strikes if needed, as they headed in the direction of their landing zone to be extracted.

If a Ranger Team was in dense jungle canopy, where a chopper couldn't land to pick them up, the extraction helicopter would be equipped with a rope ladder attached to it that would be dropped down through an opening in the canopy to the team waiting on the ground.

Ranger Team members always had a half-inch nylon rope with a steel snap link attached to their rucksack. This was used to make a rappelling seat with a square knot in front of their waist, into which they attached a 3/8-inch D-shaped steel snap link into the knot. Then three Rangers would climb up the swinging rope ladder that was attached to the hovering chopper. Once they had climbed high enough so that other team members could climb on, they snapped the steel D link over the metal rung of the rope ladder and were hoisted up out of harm's way, swinging back and forth in the air until they cleared the jungle canopy. Then they held on for life 1200 to 2000 feet above the ground while being transported to a safer location. Usually the remaining three Rangers on the ground consisted of the team leader, radio operator, and rear security, who waited for a second extraction chopper.

Once a Ranger Team's mission was compromised, they needed to be extracted. To leave a compromised Ranger Team on the ground behind enemy lines would mean certain death for the Rangers.

Extraction of a Ranger Team involved a single helicopter making a fast approach to an open landing zone, hovering a few feet off to the ground for just a brief moment. Then six Rangers ran and jumped or climbed into the chopper through the open doors on each side. It would lift off as fast as possible to avoid being hit by enemy gunfire.

The only protection the chopper had for the long few seconds of open exposure while approaching, hovering, and taking off from an open landing zone was two M-60 machine guns mounted on each side of the chopper.

At the close of the Ranger presentation, they told us we would be trained by the very best reconnaissance personnel the Army had. I had been in Vietnam about seven days and was already concerned with the drugs, attitude, and lack of discipline and respect I had observed from my fellow soldiers. I wondered if the soldiers would be the same where I was going. I wondered if I would survive. I thought for a moment and then volunteered to be a Ranger.

When I arrived at LZ English in Bong Song, Vietnam home of the 173rd Airborne Brigade and November Company 75th Airborne Rangers, who were attached to the 173rd, I'll never forget the training I received from a Hawaiian Staff Sergeant named Tad.

The first thing Tad told me was that I needed to deprogram the training I had been taught and believed in, because it was outdated and obsolete. I needed to learn new tactics in order to survive. The old training worked in World War II and Korea, but it was not relevant for Vietnam's guerilla warfare. If I used the old tactics of World War II and the Korean Conflict in Vietnam, most likely I would get myself and others killed.

In Vietnam, our enemies were experts in setting booby traps along trails and camouflaging them so we couldn't see them. They used natural things from the jungle, such as a dug-out pit with the bottom of the pit filled with sharpened sticks of bamboo or wood smeared with human feces and stuck in the ground with the sharpened end facing up ready to penetrate anything that fell into it. The dug-out pit would be completely covered and camouflaged with jungle ferns, vines, tree leaves, and branches so that it looked completely natural. They also used grenades and other explosive devices, hidden and camouflaged along a trail where we least expected one to be.

I immediately realized that the training I had received from Tad was the truth and that, in order for me to survive in Vietnam, I needed to listen, learn, and follow his teachings.

Here is one example of Tad's training compared to my state-side training: In my old training, I had been taught to always select higher ground to ambush our enemy from. But Tad taught us something totally different. He said that, while we were on a mission, we should be patient and monitor a trail to observe what direction the enemy was traveling, what types of weapons, ammo, food, and other supplies they were carrying with them.

Once we determined the enemy's direction of travel and what they were carrying, then we should set our ambush *on the right hand side* of the trail, to the enemy's direction of movement. The rationale for this kind of thinking, Tad taught us, was that most people, about 90 percent, are right handed and that the enemies' weapons would be pointed away from you as you set off the ambush.

Ambushing from the right of the trail in which the enemy is traveling, five Rangers would fire a full 20-round magazine from an M-16 rifle in 2.3 seconds. That's 100 bullets into a kill zone while the enemy freezes in shock for a second or two from all the firing. Once they realize what is happening, they fall to the ground, turning their weapons from the left to the right to locate where the firing is coming from. That just took 2.8 seconds, and, by that time, our hands would be on the detonators of five Claymore mines. Each mine has hundreds of steel buckshot packed into them with about a pound of C-4 explosives. The claymore mines explode before—the enemy can get their rifles to their shoulders to fire.

Before we ever went on a mission, Tad taught us to learn all we could about the enemy we were going up against. What size enemy forces were in the territory? What was their mission? What types of weapons were they carrying? What was their purpose for being at that location? Was a base camp nearby or were they just passing through? Without this knowledge, our chances for survival were greatly diminished.

It was up to me to choose to believe and live by Tad's teachings or to reject and not believe in the training. He told us, "Follow me. Walk where I walk. Imitate my movements, and you'll be safe." In more than 200 missions covering four years, nobody had been killed or even wounded while running missions with Tad, but he had been wounded on three different missions, receiving three Purple Hearts. He had more personal confirmed enemy kills than any other American soldier in all the Armed Services, in Vietnam. I chose to believe and obey Tad's teachings.

Tad spoke fluent Montagnard and Vietnamese. He ate what the enemy ate, he dressed just like the enemy dressed, he used the enemy's weapons, and he always walked point—out in front of his team—and they followed him.

On one mission, Tad was dressed as a North Vietnamese Regular Army soldier and was walking point for his Ranger Team when suddenly an enemy soldier spoke softly to him in Vietnamese, telling him to "Get out of the way quickly because there was an American patrol right behind him that they were going to ambush." Tad looked around, located the different enemy positions, turned to his team about ten yards behind him, and gave them the danger signal. He then turned and walked toward the enemy soldiers and opened fire, killing several enemy soldiers. Tad was wounded in both his lower legs, but no one on the team was wounded. They escaped before the enemy could regroup.

Tad taught us that one of the most important keys to survival in Vietnam was to build real, meaningful relationships with the helicopter pilots and their crews, who risked their lives to rescue us while we were in a fire-fight with an enemy that out-numbered us.

Several times I was in situations where I knew it was impossible for a chopper to break through the low ceiling of clouds in the mountainous area, but they did. Even on dark, rainy nights in the mountainous areas and under heavy gunfire, they came in and extracted us right out of the danger of death and saved our lives.

CHAPTER 2

LOST BEHIND ENEMY LINES

THERE WAS ONE Ranger mission in Vietnam when I thought we would not make it back alive. The truth is we shouldn't have survived.

We were lost—no one knew our location, we had no radio communication, we were deep in enemy territory, and we were in a fire-fight with trail watchers guarding a battalion base camp! We were outnumbered 40 to 1, and no one could hear our call for help. Only God's intervention, a miracle, saved me and my Ranger Team from certain death.

It was during the monsoon season in Vietnam. I had been in country about six months and had just returned to my Ranger Company from a week of training a South Vietnamese Airborne Ranger Team in the tactics of Ranger missions.

I was waiting to be assigned as the new Ranger Team leader for a Team. While I was waiting, the Company Commander requested that I lead a mission very close to the Cambodian border in the mountainous region of the Central Highlands. He assigned me an area of about four square miles to silently maneuver through and search for a suspected base camp that would support a battalion-sized force of North Vietnamese Army soldiers. The mountainous area had poor or no radio communication, and artillery and air support were not directly available to us. We would need to use a radio relay team or an observer plane for all our radio communications and depend on jet air strikes as our air support.

That wasn't my only concern. The Company Commander assigned five new soldiers who had just completed the two-week Ranger training course that we gave all new Ranger volunteers, and this was their first mission in Vietnam.

I expressed my concerns about going on a mission with five new soldiers who had never been on a mission before, but the Captain insisted. But he did allow me to add one experienced Ranger to my Team to help me on the mission. So I asked my best friend George, who had recently been promoted to a Team Leader position, if he would go along with me. He reluctantly agreed.

When a Ranger Team Leader receives a mission, he begins to gather the details for the mission, such as last known enemy activity, size, weapons, etc. So, the day before going on the mission, I flew a visual reconnaissance of the assigned area in an 0-1 observer plane. During this flight, I took notes on the density of the jungle, the terrain, where openings for insertion and extractions could happen, etc.

This was my first mission as Team Lead, so when I returned to the Ranger base camp after my flight, I plotted my entire mission on paper—where I wanted to be put in and how I would maneuver, where I wanted to sleep, and where we needed to be picked up at the end of our four days.

When the mission was plotted and the details worked out, I made a copy for our company's communication team, who were responsible for all our radio communication, insertion, extraction, air strikes, gunships, and any other emergency support we needed.

George and I briefed and helped our five new Ranger Team members prepare for their first mission. The following day seven of us boarded the insertion chopper, ready for our mission. The weather consisted of low gray cloud cover with occasional light rain, but the cloud cover was high enough to allow our chopper to fly into the mountainous area. Cobra gunships and another insertion chopper escorted us. This empty insertion chopper was with us as a decoy. When we were near our insertion landing zone, the decoy chopper dropped down in altitude and flew low close the ground and hovered for just a moment, simulating an insertion. The empty chopper did this several times, attempting to deceive the enemy about the true location of our landing.

As we flew toward our location, I used my compass and map and tried to follow where we were going, but I was having trouble because much of our flight was above the clouds, and I was unable to see the land markings. A half-hour into our flight, the pilot told me to get ready to get off—we were approaching the designated landing zone I had selected the day before. That's when the fun began.

As we broke through the clouds, the pilot pointed to a small landing zone, but where he pointed was not on my map. I quickly told the pilots to circle. As they did, George and I went over the terrain below, trying to pinpoint landmarks on our map, but we couldn't locate the position. The chopper pilots insisted this was the landing zone I had selected to be inserted into.

I notified my Company Commander over the radio and

explained our situation. After a brief pause, the Captain ordered me to get my Team off the chopper. I reluctantly agreed.

As the helicopter hovered over the small landing zone, we jumped off into the tall elephant grass six feet below. Ten seconds later, the chopper was off and away. We had received no enemy gunfire, so we gathered together on the side of the landing zone and tried to figure out where we were and what direction to go. After a few minutes, we realized we were truly lost. It was 10 o'clock in the morning.

On the approach to the landing zone, George had observed a finger of terrain that gradually went down into a deep gorge. We agreed to head in that direction. We needed to get away from the landing zone before any enemy arrived.

We were dressed in full jungle camouflage clothing from our flop hats to our boots. Our faces, ears, neck, and exposed hands were camouflaged. I was carrying an AK-47 with two 30-round clips taped together, one opposite the other for fast reloading.

The AK-47 is the weapon the NVA (North Vietnamese Army) and VC (Viet Cong) used. Occasionally a Ranger Team carried an AK-47, because of the distinct sound it made when fired. The "kak-kak-kak" sound of an AK-47 rifle was easily recognized compared to our usual M-16 rifle. In the event a Ranger Team wanted to fire a single shot to wound and capture a single enemy soldier, we used the AK-47 rifle to do this so our enemy wouldn't be too alarmed at a single shot from the AK. Thus, our mission wouldn't be compromised.

I took the point position, and my friend George took the rear security position, keeping the five newly trained virgin Rangers between us. The radio operator was third in line as we quietly snuck down through the thick jungle vegetation. We stopped every few minutes to make radio contact, but nobody responded.

Slowly and silently, we continued down the finger, gradually working ourselves lower, toward the narrow ravine below. The further we went, the more concerned I became about not having radio contact. I was extremely careful to observe everything the jungle allowed my eyes and ears to see and hear. I knew that, if we walked into an ambush or were spotted by an enemy soldier before I could see them, we would be in a fire-fight with an enemy force that far out-numbered us. Without radio communication, we had no way out and no fire support.

I knew our situation wasn't hopeless, because, when a Ranger Team was inserted on a mission, they were required to make radio communication checks every hour. If we missed two radio checks, back to back, a plane (an O-1 Observer) was immediately dispatched to search for and establish radio communications with the Ranger Team. The pilot of the observer plane would then determine what needed to be done to establish communications with the Ranger Team for the remainder of the mission.

I led the team carefully down the finger. At the bottom of the ravine, we came upon a small stream. Using hand motions, I signaled to the Team that I was going across the stream. It was a narrow stream—about 30 feet wide and about knee deep.

Once I crossed, I laid down on my belly and crawled up over the three-foot bank. As I spread the grassy vegetation on the top of the bank, a beaten-down path, about three feet wide, was revealed. I slowly moved my head and looked both ways on the trail, as it traveled right beside the stream. I crawled to the other side of the path and motioned for them to join me, one at a time. I detected some freshly cut wood piled beside the trail. I noticed no fish in the stream. This appeared to be the signs of an enemy camp nearby.

Once the Team was on my side of the stream, we tried again to establish radio communication, but to no avail. We checked our maps and looked at the designated area of our mission for a stream, but there were no streams in the area where we were supposed to be. George and I knew that going back to our landing zone was not a good option, because the enemy may have had an ambush waiting for us. All we could do was hope that our air support realized they had put us into the wrong area and wait for that O-1 plane to contact us—the plane was our hope.

We checked the time. It was 1 o'clock in the afternoon. We had now missed the 11 and 12 o'clock radio checks, and the third radio check was due. I knew our Ranger Company should have sent up a plane to make radio contact with us an hour earlier. Where were they? Why hadn't we heard their call for us? We knew our radio worked. We should have had communication with the pilot or at least heard the plane. I was deeply concerned. Thoughts of doubt and fear started to enter my mind.

I crawled over to George and asked for his feedback on what direction to go. George and I agreed to follow the flow of the water and stay on the beaten-down path, which went eastward. I reassumed the point position and followed the trail.

Following an enemy trail in Vietnam was extremely dangerous, because the enemy were experts at creating and hiding booby traps on trails that inflicted high casualties, killing and maiming thousands of us. However, this deep behind enemy lines, in their own territory, they usually didn't use booby traps on trails because they might kill some of their own soldiers. Instead of booby traps, the enemy utilized soldiers, hidden off the trail, as trail watchers to observe anyone approaching.

We stayed on the left-hand side of the stream and followed the flow of the water. The terrain was dense vegetation, and the land was mostly flat, with a high, impenetrable jungle canopy overhead.

After an hour of slowly sneaking along the trail, I began to hear the sound of running water. A few moments later, I could see, through the dense jungle, a large stream of fast-moving water off to our left. As I examined the dense vegetation ahead of us, I saw that the smaller stream—the one that we were following—merged into the much-larger stream. I froze, backed up a few feet, and motioned for the Team to come close together. I could feel exhaustion in my body. I looked at my Team and saw the drain and tiredness in their faces from the heat, humidity, and stress of our mission. Even with proper water intake, heat exhaustion was always a concern for Rangers, because we were carrying 45-pound rucksacks, plus all our ammo, grenades, and weapons.

When the team had grouped up, I explained what lay ahead of us: The stream we were following merged into a larger stream of water.

Our options were to cross the smaller stream to our

right, but the terrain on that side had changed from the gently sloping finger we had followed down to the stream three hours earlier to a steep incline of about 60 degrees that began immediately on the other side of the stream. The vegetation on that side was thick, and the canopy above looked like it had no openings to the sky.

Another option was for us to traverse the two streams at the point where they met and travel on the left-hand side of the bigger stream. It appeared that the trail we had been following went in that direction. I asked George for his suggestions. We decided to wade through the big stream and see what was on the other side.

It was about 2 o'clock in the afternoon. We had been on our mission for four hours, with no radio communication. But the biggest concern I now had was crossing where the trail and two streams came together. This was a no-no in the Ranger Handbook.

I was terribly uncomfortable with a new person who had never been on a mission or been in a fire-fight covering my back while I waded the stream. So I told George to come up from rear security and put his weapon on full automatic to cover me while I crossed the stream. Once I was on the other side and properly positioned, I told him I would signal for the Team to come across, one at a time.

We agreed, and I got into a low-profile position and

made my way down to where the two streams merged. The banks on both sides of the stream were about six feet high and provided some cover for me. I waded across the large stream where the depth of the water was below my waist, which kept my rucksack dry.

I crawled up over the bank on the other side and spread the vegetation to see a trail wide enough to drive a jeep on. I slowly turned my head and observed large piles of wood cut and stacked on the side of the trail and maybe twenty carved wooden gourds laid beside the trail for soldiers to get a drink of water. I carefully checked the terrain and trail both ways and decided to crawl diagonally over to the other side of the path to a rock that was large enough to hide behind and monitor the trail. I got situated in a positon behind the rock where I could see up and down the trail and see the Team on the other side. I motioned for George to come across, as I focused my attention back to the trail on my side.

All of a sudden, the *kak-kak-kak* of an AK-47 erupted from the jungle, and, in the next few seconds, my eyes went from monitoring the trail to looking back toward my Team. The first thing I noticed was George falling face first—he was in the air about halfway down to the water. I thought, *Man, what a stupid thing to do— he slipped and fell with his finger on the trigger and discharged his M-16 on full automatic. Now the whole North Vietnamese Army will be down on us.*

Then, suddenly, I realized I was seeing green tracer bullets fired in the direction of George and the rest of the team. Green tracers from an AK-47 were going all around George and into the vegetation where my Team was hiding.

I turned to see where the tracers were coming from. Surprisingly, I saw two NVA soldiers about twenty yards from me, just off the trail, standing and firing their AK-47s toward my Team. I looked back toward the Team and saw George lying in the stream. His face was floating sideways, and he wasn't moving. I thought, *Oh, no! He's dead—they got him!* I looked at the rest of the Team, no one was returning fire.

I turned around, sprang up, and fired my AK at the two soldiers. When my clip was empty I fell down behind the rock, reloaded, and fired the second 30-round clip. I dove back behind the rock. While reaching for a grenade, I looked back to my Team to get some fire support so I could come back across the stream to them.

My eyes saw George. He was back on the side with our Team members! I was relieved and happy to see him alive.

He said, "We'll cover you—come on back to our side."

As they laid down cover fire so I could return to them, I became the second human being to walk on water. Saint

Peter had done it 2000 years ago, and so did I in 1970. My feet never got wet as I flew across the stream and joined my team.

We began running up the steep 60-degree incline. It was so steep that we had to use the tree vines and smaller trees to pull ourselves up as we ran with our heavy rucksacks and gear. We were running away from what turned out to be a base camp. We could hear gunfire and yelling behind us as more enemy soldiers joined the chase after us.

As we ran up through the steep jungle incline, I though what are we going to do. We had no radio contact, I didn't know where we were, our Company didn't even know where to look for us. I thought, *Man—we're lost!* So we kept running straight uphill.

There was a large force of enemy soldiers chasing us and closing in fast. We had slowed down, we were exhausted, and we had lost all hope. We stopped and were considering setting up a defensive perimeter and making a last stand—when, suddenly, the radio operator said, "I got radio contact!" As I answered the radio, I could hear a plane way off in the distance. We gave him a compass azimuth reading from us to the plane. Hope came alive in us, like gasoline igniting on a fire. It gave us a second wind and allowed us to encourage each other to run once again.

As the pilot approached our location, we fired a red

flare up through the jungle canopy so he could see our location and direct us to a landing zone so a chopper could extract us.

The pilot spotted the flare and told us, "I got some good news and some bad news."

We responded, "Give us the good news first."

He said, "There is a small opening in the jungle canopy where I can fire a rocket into and the explosion will make a large enough hole in the canopy so that a rope ladder can be dropped to you, and you can be extracted by rope ladder." He told us that the gunships and extraction choppers were close by, because we had been reported missing for so long that they had scrambled all kinds of support to locate us and get us out.

We said, "That's awesome! It's all great news—so what's the bad news?"

A moment later the pilot came back on the radio and said, "The opening where the rope ladder can be dropped to you is about one-half mile from your current position. You need to run fast because I have an air strike on the way. Two F-4 jets with napalm will be on site in five minutes. Two more F-4s will accompany them with an air strike with bombs."

We all looked at each other. Our expectations had gone from total hopelessness to exuberant expectations for living.

I reached for my rappelling rope and steel D-link attached to my rucksack and told the team to tie a rappelling seat and hook the steel D-link into the knot so we could hook into the rope ladder and be extracted up out of the jungle canopy to safety. In less than a minute, we had our rope seats tied and inspected, and were off running, toward the tiny opening of light and life. The enemy had closed in on us, and the bullets from their burst of automatic weapons were penetrating the vegetation all around us.

Out of nowhere, Cobra gunships appeared like angels and began firing mini-guns and rockets at the enemy right behind us. We could hear the mini-gun bullets whiz through the vegetation just above our heads. The pilot in that little O-1 observer plane had directed their fire onto the enemy with pinpoint accuracy.

We ran for about five minutes; then we spotted a small hole in the canopy—rays of light shone all the way to the jungle floor. Before we even got under the small hole, a voice on the radio said, "Here's your lifeline." We looked up and watched as a rope ladder fell right out of the sky, to the ground. It swayed back and forth in slow motion. The voice on the radio said, "Hurry—send four up the ladder, have them hook in, and hang on. We'll send another ladder for the three who remain." George and I stayed behind with the radio operator. We turned and started firing at the enemy behind us.

A minute later, while still receiving enemy fire, the second rope ladder fell from heaven. The three of us were on it and hooked up in record time. As it lifted us up through the thick jungle canopy, we could see and hear the air strike of napalm land on the base camp back at the stream we crossed. We could see the Cobra gunships firing their mini-guns into the enemy who had been chasing us.

The chopper rose high up into the sky and began its journey to take us back to the safety of our base camp. We were about 1500 feet above the ground, traveling at about 120 miles per hour on a rope ladder that hung down below the chopper about 30 to 40 feet. A steady stream of tears flowed from my eyes—partially from the wind in my face and mostly from my heart as I realized what God had just done. I looked at the ½-inch rope that secured me to the 1-inch aluminum rung on the rope ladder that hung back behind the chopper like a cape. I asked myself, "God, how did you save us? Why did you save us?" I hung on for dear life.

We made it back to the Ranger compound safely. After the debriefing, George and I sat alone, both of us in total awe of how God had spared our lives. We both knew that our survival was a true miracle from God. We were near exhaustion, we were lost, we had lost all hope of living, and were ready to give up, when we got the call.

It was a miracle that the plane located us at just the right second, that the gunships were already on their way, that the extraction choppers—not one, but two—were sent equipped with rope ladders already attached, to extract us. How did they know?

It was God's grace and mercy that allowed us to escape certain death. I say by God's grace and mercy because I had been brought up by a mother who feared, loved, and obeyed God. She brought me up, from a baby, in a Bible-believing church. When I was 13, I was looking at Bible colleges to attend after high school, to become the next Billy Graham.

But, in my freshman year of high school, I decided to trade in my loyalty to God for high school popularity, girls, sports, and being accepted by my new friends in the world. I ran away from God and cheated on Him. My relationship with God changed. God wanted to have a relationship with me, but I just wanted to have an affair with God whenever I needed Him. I acted like I was happy and like everything was great with my new life, but it wasn't. I knew the truth: I had turned my back on God. That's why I say that it was only by God's grace and mercy that I am alive, whole, and with a sound mind.

Why did God's grace and mercy surround me during my 18 months in Vietnam, providing me ways to escape death more times than I care to remember? Why did God do it for me and not for others?

Because my mother believed that God would honor her prayers and take care of her son, whom she had named after the Old Testament prophet Daniel, who had survived one night in the lion's den.

Even though I was a horrible sinner who had turned my back on God, His provisions of grace and mercy allowed me to be trained by Tad, an expert in guerilla warfare, so I would survive all the death traps that Satan had planned to use to kill, maim, and destroy me.

All the drugs, alcohol, snakes, jungle animals, fire-fights, enemy booby traps, ambushes, trail watchers, and snipers, all the enemy schemes to kill me, God allowed me to survive. Because of my mother, my sister, and my brother's prayers and God's grace and mercy! But why? Because He had a purpose and mission for me!

I came back home from Vietnam alive, with hardly a scratch on my body, while more than 58,267 American soldiers were killed in action, 303,644 American soldiers were wounded in action, and more than 1,500 soldiers were missing in action.

Physical warfare is real. The enemy we faced was real. There were thousands of them who believed in what they were taught and acted on their belief. They were experts at guerilla warfare, the best in the world. Their bullets were real.

This physical war really happened. We saw it, we heard it, and we felt the effects of physical war in Vietnam. I witnessed it. Land was conquered, and a new nation was born.

CHAPTER 3

KNOW YOUR ENEMY

IN VIETNAM WHEN I went on a reconnaissance mission, I needed to know how my enemy operated, what they had for weapons, what they were trying to accomplish, and what weapons I needed to accomplish my mission successfully.

In physical warfare, you take territory, you wound and kill others, or get wounded and killed. You capture prisoners of war or become a prisoner of war.

Your survival depends on the relationships you establish, the reality of the training you receive, your believing in the training, and your effective use of the training.

Warfare is not a game. If you allow your mind, body,

and heart to be influenced by anything other than your readiness for action, your chances of survival are greatly reduced.

Spiritual warfare is much the same as physical warfare. But many people are unaware of the spirit world and ask, "Is the spiritual realm real?" The answer is, "Yes, the spiritual realm is a real, yet unseen existence, alive and active."

However, spiritual life is not understood by even the wisest of humans because we have a flesh body. The senses in our physical body do not have the ability to operate in the spiritual world, unless God permits us supernaturally and spiritually to do so, or unless you are controlled by the devil.

Humans cannot hear, feel, and see in the spiritual realm. So, because we can't see, hear, or touch, we don't think about it, and some people don't even believe that a spiritual life exists. They don't believe a spiritual war is going on right now. They believe it's a figment of someone's imagination.

Their believing or not believing doesn't change the fact that there really is a war going on right now with Satan and his demonic spirits (Evil) against God, His angels, and praying saints (Good). Every day we are constantly being influenced, set up, tempted, ambushed, and attacked by evil spirits.

Satan is in control of the world. He is the prince of this world today and will be until Jesus Christ returns at the end of the tribulation period. This is why the Disciple John told us, "We know that we are children of God, and that the whole world is under the control of the evil one." (I John 5:19)

We must understand and recognize that the very air about us is filled with hostile forces that have succeeded in keeping you from having a relationship with God.

For those who are God's children, Satan is constantly attempting to destroy our fellowship with God and to deprive us and cut us off from the source that nourishes us.

This war is for the possession of your soul. The battleground is your mind, your will, your emotions; the purpose of the conflict from Satan's perspective is to dominate your unredeemed soul. "For our struggle is not against flesh and blood, but against the rulers, against the authorities, against the powers of this dark world and against the spiritual forces of evil in the heavenly realms." (Ephesians 6:12)

Human beings who do not believe in Jesus as the Messiah and people who say they believe in Jesus but live a lifestyle of sin are under the spiritual control and influence of the prince of this world, Satan, and his demonic angels, and the principalities and powers of darkness.

Most of the people under the influence and control of

Satan are unaware that they are children of the wicked one. They don't realize their spiritual father is Satan, which makes them enemies of God.

Satan and his sinful nature, which possess us at birth, truly is more powerful than any human being, until we ask Jesus to become our savior and live in us.

Satan, whose aliases are "The Serpent," "The Wicked One," and "The Devil," is a created being, a fallen cherub (angel) who became twisted on the inside. Satan was a very powerful arch- angel named Lucifer, serving God before he was cast out of heaven.

The Devil's power source is us. When we believe his lies, our believing empowers him and makes us slaves to his spiritual control. We are born from our mother's womb with a sinful nature already in us, born as children of the Wicked one, the Devil. He's in full control of us and most of us don't even realize we are deeply enslaved to his dark world. This is how slick and devious Satan is.

Jesus told us Satan was "a murderer from the beginning, not holding to the truth, for there is no truth in him. When he lies, he speaks his native language, for he is a liar and the father of lies." (John 8:44)

The Devil and his evil followers are always trying to draw you and me away from our Heavenly Father, trying to destroy our relationship with God, thus disrupting the goodness of what God has planned for our lives.

Pride is one of the most powerful and popular weapons Satan uses on humans—and we love it. The reason pride is such a powerfully deceptive spiritual weapon is that pride blinds us from the reality that we even need God. We become full of ourselves, blind to our creator and our need to be filled with God's Holy Spirit.

Pride tells us we can do things without God's help or intervention. Through pride, we become blinded, hard-hearted, and rebellious, opposing God. Pride convinces us we have no need of God. When blinded with pride, we believe Satan's lies and think we are okay.

Unless God breaks us down to a point where we humble ourselves, Satan will continue to destroy us. God is the turning point, the turning-around place! We need God's help! We need God!

The sole purpose of Satan and his forces is two-fold:

1) To keep non-believers from hearing the Good News and truth about Jesus and believing it. He will do anything legal or illegal to stop a human being from getting into a relationship with Jesus.

2) For those who believe in Jesus as their savior, Satan will do anything to maim us, to inflict wounds on us, and to discourage us, so we will lose heart and fall out of fellowship with the Father.

Once the relationship breaks down just a little bit, and we slack off on our praying and our reading, and our relationship with God becomes strained, we start blaming God for our circumstances, sickness, financial problems, and broken marriages.

Then Satan, like a lion, stalks us, and, when he finds us weak enough, he tries to separate us even more. We become like a single prey, separated from the rest of the group. We stop our relationship with God and are fully exposed to the lion. We are very vulnerable at this point spiritually.

This is a "Kill Zone." The Disciple Peter told us, "Be self-controlled and alert. Your enemy the devil prowls around like a roaring lion looking for someone to devour. Resist him, standing firm in the faith, because you know that your brothers throughout the world are undergoing the same kind of sufferings." I Peter 5:8-9

CHAPTER 4

PRISONERS OF WAR

THOUGHT GOD CREATED the world and was in control of everything.

How did this spiritual war begin?

How did Satan become our spiritual father and in control of us?

Before God created the planet Earth, God created the angels as spiritual beings, with intelligence, emotions, and a will. All the angels were holy and righteous and had diverse shapes, sizes, names, and different responsibilities. They lived with God in the height of heaven, performing worship and enjoying being around the glory of God.

God put one of the powerful Cherub angels into an exalted position right over the throne of the universe and named him Lucifer. Lucifer was created as the model of perfection, full of wisdom and exquisite in beauty. He was adorned with every precious stone beautifully crafted and set in the finest gold, given to him on the day God created him.

God ordained and anointed him as the mighty angelic guardian. He had access to God's holy mountain, and he walked among the stones of fire. Lucifer was blameless in all that he did until the day evil was found in him. Everything created by God in the heavens, including angelic beings, was holy, righteous, and good, until *evil was found in Lucifer.*

Lucifer's pride caused him to devise a plan to ascend into heaven and assault God's throne above the stars of God.

Lucifer accepted this plan in his heart:

> I will ascend to the heavens;
> I will raise my throne above the stars of God;
> I will sit enthroned on the mount of assembly, on the utmost heights of Mount Zaphon;
> I will ascend above the tops of the clouds;
> I will make myself like the Most High.

Just after God created the Earth, but before He created human beings, pride overcame Lucifer. His plan was to lead one-third of heaven's angels in an all-out assault on God's throne and rule everything by forcibly taking control of God's throne.

Lucifer and his host of angels, who chose to disobey God's structure of creation by assaulting His throne, *became evil and sinful angels*, opposing God and enemies of God, who is Holy. It is impossible for Evil—Lucifer and his forces, (one-third of the host of all heavenly angels) to exist with holiness.

War broke out in heaven. Archangel Michael and his angels went to battle with Lucifer, also known as The Red Dragon, and his angels. Lucifer and his forces of evil angels were defeated. There was no room for them in heaven any longer.

So, Lucifer was cast down and out of heaven. He and the evil, unclean angels, who supported him in his rebellion against God, were literally ejected from God's throne with all the quickness and power of lightning. They were cast down to planet Earth.

They were confined and restrained to planet Earth and the atmospheric heaven around Earth, by the command of God's Word.

When Lucifer was cast out of heaven to Earth, he was never again called "Lucifer." He became the seducer—the deceiver of all humanity. His name changed. That age-old serpent became known by several other names, including the *Serpent, Satan,* meaning *"the Accuser,"* *"the Evil one,"* and *"the Devil."* This all occurred before humanity was created.

God then created Adam and Eve "to rule over the fish in the sea, the birds in the sky, over the livestock and all the wild animals, and over all the creatures that move along the ground." We were created to be God's representatives here on planet Earth. (Genesis 1:26-27)

God, who is Spirit, is holy, righteous, and pure. He originally created us in His image and likeness. We were created a *spirit* being with a *body* of flesh that was holy, righteous, and pure, without sin. We were also created with an *eternal soul* to live forever and had a *free will* to choose what we wanted.

The purpose of man's **spirit** is to communicate with God's Spirit and in turn communicate what God's Holy Spirit says to *our* soul and body.

Our **body** of flesh contains the spirit and soul of man as long as the body remains alive. Our **mind** is part of our body and functions only in the physical realm.

Our body of flesh is sensitive to the "things of the flesh" and natural physical surroundings—for example, sight, hearing, smell, touch, and taste.

The body sends all its information regarding the senses,

emotions, desires, and needs, to the mind. The mind gathers information and articulates to the soul what the body wants. (Initially, at creation, every thought function that went through Adam and Eve's mind was holy, righteous, and pure. It was all "good," because no evil existed in humanity at that "time)."

Our **soul,** also known as the heart of man, is also confined in the body. The soul of man is the real me and you—our personalities, likes, dislikes, and attitudes.

The Soul of Man is the referee or the decision-making part of us humans. The soul decides either to go with what man's spirit communicates to the soul, which is from God, or the soul could decide to go with what the body communicates, through the mind, to it. This process of decision making we refer to as our *free will.*

Our **free will** is an independent free will—free to choose, to say, and to do what we desire to do. Even when we choose to disobey God, He honors our will because He created us in His image and likeness and is bound by His standards of creation, therefore, God must honor our choices.

Today our body is addicted to many different things and is in control of many people's lives. It's the body that is in control and dictates to the soul what it wants. The body is influenced by the "senses of the flesh." (However, this is not the way God created us. He created us to be in control—with our soul—and dictate to the flesh what to do.)

Initially, God's intentions were clear. He gave Adam and Eve and their descendants dominion and authority over the entire Earth and all creation. God put Adam here to be His representative on earth. "The highest heavens belong to the LORD, but the Earth he has given to man." (Psalms 115:16)

God didn't give *ownership* of the Earth to humanity, but He assigned the responsibility of governing planet Earth to humanity. Adam was God's governor on Earth.

God put His very life and Spirit into us. He communed with us; we were His children, and He was our Father. Adam had a direct relationship with God, and Adam enjoyed being in the Garden of Eden in God's presence. God told Adam, "You are free to eat from any tree in the garden; but you must not eat from the tree of the knowledge of good and evil, for when you eat of it you will surely die." (Genesis 2: 16-17)

God wanted a family of sons and daughters who could personally relate to Him, and He to them. So He created our original parents, Adam and Eve, with the ability to reproduce spiritual beings, in exactly their likeness. "Has not the LORD made them one? In flesh and spirit, they are his. And why one? Because he was seeking godly offspring." (Malachi 2:15)

Sin and its **rebellious sinful nature** entered the

human race when Satan masqueraded as a serpent, who was craftier than any of the animals God had made. Satan deceived Eve into eating the fruit from the "Tree of Knowledge of Good and Evil," and she gave some to Adam to eat. The moment Adam ate the forbidden fruit, Satan's rebellious sinful nature entered their bodies.

God is Spirit, is holy, and cannot coexist with sin. So God removed His Spirit from the human race. This is not what God intended or the way He created us.

God had no choice but to remove Adam and Eve from the Garden of Eden, before they ate fruit from the **"Tree of Life."**

If Adam and Eve would have eaten from the "Tree of Life" after they had sinned, the human race would live forever in the state of sin that they were in. There would have been no way for God to redeem us. No way for the remission of sin. So, God drove Adam and Eve quickly from the garden.

When Adam and Eve sinned, we lost our relationship with God; the ability to walk and talk with God was gone. The peace and joy were gone. The loving closeness was gone. His Holy Spirit was removed *resulting in the loss of our relationship with God.*

The very purpose and meaningfulness to God was shattered. God created us for the purpose of having a righteous relationship with His Children without sin. Now a discrepancy existed between who God had created us to be and who we had become. All because Adam and Eve chose to believe Satan over God.

Many of us don't understand the impact that Adam and Eve's sin had. Until God spoke in Genesis 3:19, there was no physical death for humans. We were not created to die. But, sin brought God's covenant of physical death to us, and, more importantly, sin provoked the removal of God's Holy Spirit from dwelling in us, which resulted in a severing of our relationship with God, causing spiritual death.

Today, as a result of Adam and Eve's sin, every human being produced from the seed of man and born from the womb of woman is born with a rebellious sinful nature. The Bible says, *"When Adam sinned, sin entered the world. Adam's sin brought death, so death spread to everyone, for everyone sinned."* Romans 5:12

Sin also caused Adam the loss of his earthly representation status. The authority that God entrusted to Adam over planet Earth was so complete and final that Adam had the ability to give it away—and that is exactly what happened when Adam chose to sin against God. Adam ended up giving away to Satan the authority that God had delegated to Adam, affecting and *infecting* the entire human race.

Satan used this authority when he offered it to Jesus when He was in the wilderness fasting. Satan approached Jesus and took Him high up and showed Him all the kingdoms of the world in an instant. Satan told Jesus, "I will give you all their authority and splendor; for it is mine to give to whomever I want to, if you but bow down and worship me." (Luke 4:5-6) Jesus didn't argue with Satan. Jesus knew that Satan had deceived Eve and received the authority from Adam.

Why is God so opposed to Sin? Because the price we must pay for our sin is being separated from God spiritually, meaning we are spiritually dead to God while we are alive on Earth. From the moment of sin in the Garden of Eden until today, "we have all sinned and fallen short of the glory of God." And, "the wages of sin is death." (Romans 3:23 and 6:23)

Sin keeps us separated from God. Yet God's love desires our redemption.

Where does this leave us today? People today are not concerned about their separation from God. We have no thoughts about eternity and life after we die. The most important thing to us is living, and we believe that, once death occurs, life stops.

We don't think about life after death in the spiritual realm. We are not prepared for it, and many of us don't even care. The world we live in has convinced us that we are just fleshy human bodies and that all there really is to life is what's on this earth. So "Enjoy life to the fullest" is our motto.

Many feel it isn't fair for God to judge us because of Adam's sin. Yet, each of us has the same sinful rebellious nature and frequently sin against God each day. All of us are guilty and have inherited Adam's sinful rebellious nature, the tendency to sin, and God's punishment for sin, which is death.

Today the powers of sin are stronger than we are. We have become enslaved in a sinful nature. Jesus said, "I tell you the truth: everyone who sins is a slave to sin." (John 8:34) Apostle Paul, speaking of the spiritual power of sin, tells us "the whole world is a prisoner to sin." (Galatians 3:22)

"I know that nothing good lives in me, that is, in my sinful nature. For I have the desire to do what is good, but I cannot carry it out." (Romans 7:18)

"For the sinful nature desires what is contrary to the Spirit and the Spirit what is contrary to the sinful nature. They are in conflict with each other, so that you do not do what you want." (Galatians 5:17)

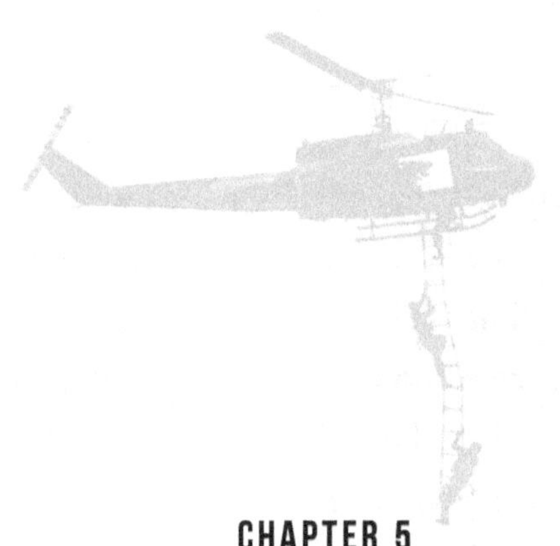

CHAPTER 5

ONLY ONE WAY OUT

Wouldn't it be nice if we could start our lives all over again and re-establish our relationship with God? God and sin cannot co-exist. So, somehow our rebellious sinful nature, along with all our sins, would need to be removed from us, before God's Holy Spirit could once again dwell in us, like He did in the Garden of Eden.

The only hope and source of power over sin and Satan is Jesus, the Only Begotten Son of God. This is why He came from eternity to planet Earth. Jesus is all about God's love and His provision of forgiveness for us. Jesus said, "I am the way, the truth, and the life. No one can come to the Father except through me." (John 14:6)

It all began 2000 years ago. It was about 9:00 in the morning when they nailed His hands and feet to the wooden cross and hung Him up in the air above the ground on a hill named Calvary.

Jesus had received no rest the night before; the Roman soldiers whipped Him horribly on His back and sides with a leather whip equipped with a metal barb-tip on the end designed to cut to the bone and rip the flesh from his body. They punched Him with their fists, kicked Him, beat Him with wooden staffs, crowned Him with a crown of thorns, and mocked Him as they hung a purple cape on His back and called Him "King of the Jews." Jesus was already near death as a result of the blood he shed from the wounds He had received during the night.

Satan began his victory dance. He had tried several times to kill Jesus, but somehow Jesus had always escaped. Now it had finally happened. Satan was extremely happy—he had achieved his goal: he has Jesus, "the Only Begotten Son of God," right where he wanted him, nailed to the cross, prepared for death.

The day Jesus was crucified was the first day of Passover; this was a very special week of festivities for the Jews. The Jewish law required all activity to cease by the end of the day. So these crucifixions needed to be completed, the bodies off the crosses, and into the tombs, by 6:00 P.M.

The Passover is in celebration of God delivering the children of Israel and Moses out from the bondage of Egyptian slavery.

1500 years after Moses led the Children of Israel out from the bondage of Egyptian slavery, on exactly the same day, Jesus was led out of the city of Jerusalem to be sacrificed in our place.

Satan didn't have a clue that God had orchestrated this spectacular plan of sending His only son Jesus to Earth to take our death sentence by shedding His blood and dying in our place as a one-time, perfect sacrifice. To pay the ransom price for all human sin—so we could be forgiven and set free from the bondage of sin, that Satan had us bound to.

As a result of being beaten all night, Jesus' body was ready for death sooner than the two criminals who were crucified with Him. It was about 3:00 o'clock in the after-noon as Jesus breathed out His last breath. He cried out, "*It is finished,*" *(Telestai)* and immediately He "gave up His Spirit."

Two thousand years ago, *Telestai* meant to bring something to completion, to finalize something, as the word "finished" implies. At the time Jesus was crucified, the word *Telestai* was also used on financial invoices and contracts where money was owed. It was written on or stamped *Telestai*, meaning the **account is paid in full.**

When Jesus cried out, "It is finished," Jesus was not talking about His death. Jesus was talking about *the authority* of *Hell* and *death* that Satan held over the human race. That's what was "finished." It was taken from Satan by Jesus.

All of a sudden, as Jesus breathed out His last breath and said, "It is finished," an intense spiritual war broke out. Satan thought his plan to kill Jesus had been successful, but now, Satan realized he had made the biggest blunder of his reign on planet Earth—a mistake that he would never recover from. He was ensnared in an ambush that would condemn, paralyze, and destroy his principalities and powers of darkness over the human race, and there was no way out for him. Satan was irate!

The spiritual battle became so violent that it manifested into the physical: the earth shook violently, so much so that the tombs broke open and the bodies of many holy saints came to life. The rocks split, and, when the Roman soldiers saw this, they were terrified and cried out. "Surely He was the Son of God!" (Read Matthew 27:50-54)

Satan thought he had successfully planned the death of Jesus. But now his stronghold, the principalities of darkness, and his spiritual contract over humanity had been voided by the blood of Jesus! God's new will took place right before Satan's eyes, and there was nothing he could do about it.

Shortly after Jesus died, the Roman soldiers broke the legs of the two criminals who were crucified with Him to ensure they would die quickly. The reason for breaking the legs was to stop them from using their legs to push themselves up to breathe. Once the legs were broken, the pain was too severe to push themselves up, so they would suffocate and die sooner.

When they came to Jesus, He appeared to be dead, so, instead of breaking His legs, one of the Roman soldiers took his spear and drove it up into Jesus' body, piercing the heart. Blood and water flowed out of His heart; the soldier did this to ensure that Jesus was dead. They needed to have the dead bodies off the crosses and into their graves before the end of the day.

Jesus' dead body was laid in a borrowed tomb, but that's not where the story ends. Jesus' spirit was alive and took the curse of death, along with our sins, sicknesses, and diseases, into Hell and left them there, where they belonged.

Because God's children are human beings—made of flesh and blood—the Son also became flesh and blood. For only as a human being could he die, and only by dying could he break the power of the devil, who had the power of death. Only in this way could he set free all who had lived their lives as slaves to the fear of dying. (Hebrews 2:14-15 NLT)

Satan had the power to control the "Gates of Hell," so, no souls escaped without his permission. Jesus destroyed Satan's principalities, his powers, and his stronghold over humanity, removing the spiritual barriers that had existed since Adam and Eve had sinned in the Garden of Eden.

Jesus set the captives and the saints free from Satan's imprisonment in Hades. On the third day, when Jesus heard God's cry for Him, He hurled back Satan and the demonic forces of darkness—and the awful burden of sin, diseases, and sickness—that He had carried there. Early that Sunday morning, when Jesus came up out of Hades, He arose back to life and brought with Him the imprisoned saints of old that He had set free.

Jesus defeated death and the grave by dying and returning from death to live again. When He did, "the tombs broke open. The bodies of many godly men and women who had died were raised from the dead. They left the cemetery after Jesus' resurrection, went into the holy city of Jerusalem, and appeared to many people. (Matthew 27:52-53)

When Jesus arose, He said, "I am the Living One; I was dead, and behold I am alive forever and ever! And I hold the keys of death and Hades." (Revelations 1:18 NIV)

Today, Jesus stands before Heaven, Earth, and Hell, as our Medal of Honor winner, **our Secret Weapon,** and undisputed victor over man's ancient destroyer, Satan, sin, and separation from God.

Please understand that Jesus' defeat of Satan, his forces, and his works affects only those who love, believe, and obey Jesus' teachings and have been born of God's Holy Spirit.

If you don't believe in God's Son Jesus—or if you say you believe but are living a lifestyle of sin—you belong to Satan, and you are an enemy of God.

Jesus loved us so much that He willingly left His glorious throne in Heaven to come to planet Earth knowing He had to endure all the punishment, hate, shame, pain, curses, and death of crucifixion on a cross—a death sentence that was reserved for only the lowest of humans.

He could have stopped it when they started beating Him. He could have called down a host of angels when they were whipping the flesh off His back. He could have commanded them to stop before they began to drive the nails into His wrists. But He didn't. Jesus died for us, because He loves so very much and wants us to establish a loving, obedient relationship with Him and Father God.

Jesus made the first choice—to love and die for us, to invite us to live with Him forever. We make the next choice: either to accept or reject His offer. Without Jesus dying for us, we would have no choice to make.

It is up to us. We get to choose where we spend eternity, in Heaven or Hell.

If we answer God's call and accept Jesus, then we begin a new life by establishing a new relationship.

Our relationship with God the Father is through Jesus Christ, and **it is conditional** based on two critical teachings of Jesus.

1) Our belief, what we believe while alive on Earth, will determine our destination in eternity.

2) Our behaviour and actions, while alive on Earth, will determine our rewards in Heaven or our retribution we receive in Hell.

So, I ask you this question: Do you have a loving relationship with Jesus and Father God?

A relationship demands constant change and work to keep it alive, growing, and maturing, in all areas. A relationship is open, based on truth, respect, trust, obedience, and a love that desires to please the one we love.

Or are you trying to have *an affair with God*?

An affair is secretive, selfish, and based on seduction to benefit and please one's own pleasures. An affair is temporal and thrives on emotional highs, gifts, and greed.

God demands a relationship from us and will turn down an affair! An affair will not make it!

CHAPTER 6

A RELATIONSHIP, NOT AN AFFAIR

IN VIETNAM, I had the best training available. I built a relationship with my Ranger Mentor Tad, who was an expert in guerilla warfare. It was my choice whether to listen, learn, believe, and obey Tad's teachings or to reject them.

I chose to listen to him. I acted like him; I ate what he ate. I walked like he walked, I talked like he talked, I camouflaged my face, neck, ears, and arms like he did, I dressed like he dressed and I thought and meditated on all kinds of situations that might occur while on a mission, so we could react and survive when outnumbered by the enemy.

If I had established a friendly affair with Tad and his teachings in Vietnam, I would have been like many other Rangers who were killed or wounded because they failed to establish **a relationship** with Tad. Instead they just had a casual *friendly affair* with him. They listened to all his teachings but used only the teachings and trainings that they liked—the ones that excited and benefited them. However, when something went wrong or they were in trouble and needed advice, they always turned to Tad to fix it.

In today's world, many of us who call ourselves Christians turn to God when we think we have a problem, but the problem we think we have may not be what God sees as our problem. We may think our problem is money, but God sees our problem as **sin**. Sin must be brought to God first. We must repent, from our heart, of our sins against God and ask Him to forgive us.

Have you ever had someone do something that hurt you mentally or physically and then tell you they're sorry and asked you to forgive them? But you knew they didn't really mean what they said when they asked you to forgive them. They just needed you to do something for them, so they were just seeking to patch things up so that they could continue being benefited by your relationship.

That's exactly what many people do today when they come to God and ask to be saved. They confess with their emotions and mind because they want God to do something for them *but don't mean it in their hearts.*

Each one of us individually must establish our own meaningful relationship with Christ Jesus. The only way to establish a relationship with God is to crawl up on the cross at Calvary and die to our sinful nature.

The minute we were born from our mother's womb, we were slaves to Satan and sin, making us children of the wicked one and enemies of God. Once we choose to serve God as our new master, we must surrender and die to our sinful nature and become a Ranger in the army of Jesus serving the Kingdom of Heaven.

What happens to most of us is that we get up on the cross and stay for a while. We make an emotional commitment to God because we needed something. So we tell God we're sorry, but we really don't mean it. Then, at the first sign of strife, hardship, or sorrow, we crawl off the cross with our sinful nature—still alive. *We didn't die.* We went to the cross because we needed God to do something for us. We made a deal—but we didn't really mean it.

Some of us do this again and again. We stay on the cross long enough to suffer some, but we don't die to the sinful nature. Just before we give up and die to the pleasures of the flesh, our talking past whispers in our ears—reminding us of the pleasures of sin. So we jump off the cross.

It took me 40 years of being on and off the cross. I went on and off the cross so many times, I must have set a record in Heaven. I just didn't want to die to the sinful nature.

Sometimes I went there and told God, "If you get me out of this mess, I'm yours. I'll do what you want me to do, I'll obey you." But I didn't really mean it from my heart. After a while, I was afraid to go to Jesus anymore, because I had been there so many times and failed Him. Every time I came to Jesus, my past would tell me I didn't mean it, that I wasn't strong enough to live up to my commitment, and that I'd fail again.

Then one day, I felt, deep inside me, shame, sorrow, and regret, and I knew it was the pain of repentance. Also present was a boldness and deep desire to change my way of living. God had finally broken my contrite spirit. I spiritually surrendered my will and repented from my heart of my sinful nature and lifestyle that I had lived against Him.

This time, I stayed on the cross until I surrendered and died to the old sinful nature. We must all die on the cross at Calvary to our old sinful nature and accept Jesus. Apostle Paul tells us, "I have been crucified with Christ and I no longer live, but Christ lives in me. The life I live in the body, I live by faith in the Son of God, who loved me and gave himself for me." (Galatians 2:20)

One picture firmly imprinted in my memory from Vietnam is that of an enemy soldier who had been captured as a prisoner of war. He had surrendered holding a pacification pamphlet, dropped from an aircraft, that guaranteed them that if they surrendered, they would receive a new life of freedom.

When the enemy soldier *surrendered,* he did it with both his hands and arms held straight up high into the air—in total surrender. In his eyes was extreme fear. He shook all over; he wet himself. He came with a humble, meek, and fearful attitude. It took faith for him to surrender because his life depended on us keeping our **word** to him. He had enough faith to trust us with his life. He surrendered and meant it from his heart.

He knew that, when he gave up, his old lifestyle was gone, and whatever life he had left to live, he would serve a new master, living a new life.

Today, when we tell God, "I give you my life," we need to surrender just like the prisoners of war did in Vietnam—and mean it from our hearts.

This is how it looks: We turn away from our old sinful lifestyle and face our Medal of Honor Winner Jesus, walk to the cross, kneel down, and give him our life full of sin, wounds, and scars. We give him everything—all our baggage. We lay it down at the feet of Jesus in total surrender. Jesus' blood cleanses us from all our sins, all shame, and all unrighteousness and then removes all the spiritual scar tissue and heals all our wounds.

Then, Jesus presents us—holy, righteous, and pure—to His Father, so that we can have a relationship with Him and Father God.

I believe the greatest word in the English language is the word *redeem*. Redeem means "to buy back"; another meaning is "to save from captivity by paying a ransom."

You must understand that, for us to be free from the deadly consequences of our sins, a tremendous price had to be paid—a price we are unable and cannot pay. The only thing superior to us is God the Father and His Only Begotten Son, Jesus.

God chose to buy us back by offering His Son, Jesus, in exchange for our lives. This is why the shedding of Jesus' blood on the Cross is vital. Nothing on Earth is as important as our having a relationship with God. Everything you expect God to do for you *is conditional on your relationship with Him.* Just surrender.

Today, I have the privilege of introducing you to the Only Begotten Son of God, Jesus, who gave His life for you and me. He was raised from death's tomb back to life, never to die again. Instead, He ascended into heaven, where He now sits on His Father's throne.

Please welcome into your hearts Jesus, the Messiah, your Secret Weapon and ***Savior.*** He loves you and wants you to establish a relationship with Him.

It's your choice. You must choose Jesus as your master while you're alive here on Earth.

If you don't choose Jesus, you will live your life on Earth *separated from God.* **If** you die chained to those burdens of sin and Satan, you'll spend eternity in the deepest darkness you have ever witnessed: The Home of Satan—called Hell. You will be separated from God forever, and ever, and ever.

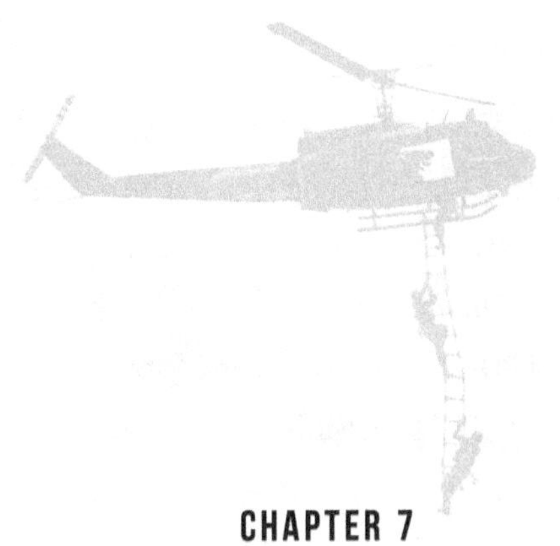

CHAPTER 7

PEACE TREATY MEDIATED BY BLOOD

JESUS' MISSION WAS to provide "the way" for all peoples of all nations to have "the right" to become Children of God, by believing in Him and all that He is.

And that's exactly what Jesus did on the Cross at Calvary. He was the intercessor—the go-between for God and humanity.

He mediated a Peace Treaty between the sinful human race and God. But that's not all Jesus did, He also stepped in between Satan and mankind as an intercessor for the human race.

Whenever I think of Jesus interceding for us at Calvary as our mediator, it reminds me of a scripture and a story that may help you remember this teaching on reconciliation. Author *Dutch Sheets*, in his book *Intercessory Prayer*, calls this the "Bear Anointing" story.

In Proverbs 17:12, the Bible says, *"Better to meet a bear robbed of her cubs than a fool in his folly."*

I have never met a Momma bear in the Maine woods with her cubs, and I hope I never do. But a wise old Maine woodsman once taught me the art of surviving bear encounters when he gave me this piece of advice. "Son, try to avoid bears at all cost. But if you can't, and it's a female that you have run into, don't ever intercede or get in between Momma bear and her cubs.

Because, if you do, there's fixing to be a meeting, and you're going to be on the receiving end of the meeting. It'll be downright ferocious."

Mediation and intercession involves delegation and authority, and it can be violent.

Intercession requires a meeting, and there were two different intercessory meetings that took place at Calvary, both involving Jesus, and both helped make the Peace Treaty viable.

The first intercessory meeting Jesus had at Calvary was with Satan. It was violent and ugly. Satan had come between God and His "cubs." He should never have done that, because after 4000 years of pent-up fury, Jesus interceded on our behalf in the meeting of all meetings.

Satan's worst nightmares came true at Calvary. The sky grew dark, the earth shook, rocks split in two, the graves were opened, and many bodies of the saints who had fallen asleep were raised. All this happened as

Love met hate,

goodness met evil,

light met darkness,

righteousness met sin, and

truth met lies.

This was a disuniting meeting between Satan and humanity. Satan's strongholds, principalities, powers, and headship over mankind was destroyed. Jesus took the keys of death and the grave away from Satan.

The second intercessory meeting at Calvary took place as Jesus hung between God and humanity on the Cross. This was a uniting meeting, providing the entire human race a right and a way to become reconciled to Father God. This mediation was good and pleasant for humanity and God.

But, for Jesus, this meeting was very difficult. It killed Him. Jesus became our scape-goat, bearing all our sins, diseases, illnesses, and addictions. All the sinful bondage that Satan had us bound and shackled to was heaved onto Jesus as he interceded on the Cross between God and humans.

As a result of Jesus' blood and intercession for us on the Cross at Calvary, a **Peace Treaty** was put into effect, in which *Mercy and truth have met together; Righteousness and peace have kissed.* (Psalms 85:10 NKJV)

Only God could plan such an event and have it turn out perfect. God's New Will, **"The New Covenant,"** went into effect at Calvary. Apostle Paul tells us, *"Therefore, since we have been justified through faith, we have peace with God through our Lord Jesus Christ."* Romans 5:1 NIV

I find it fascinating that the Serpent Satan, who accomplished his greatest victory in the Garden of Eden from a tree, *The Tree of Knowledge of Good and Evil,* also suffered his greatest defeat from a tree—*the **Cross at Calvary**.*

When we **turn** from our wicked ways, **repent** of our sins, and **believe** in Jesus, we are set free. The removal of our sins is not a process. **It is done immediately.**

The Bible says, *"He has removed our sins as far from us as the east is from the west."* Psalms 103:12 NLT version

Paul tells us, *"Therefore, if anyone is in Christ, he is a new creation; old things have passed away; behold, all things have become new.*" II Corinthians 5:17 NKJV

Children born of God will not continue to deliberately, knowingly, and habitually practice sin. Because we have been born of God, His seed remains in us, and we cannot go on sinning. (I John 3:9)

But if anybody does sin, *we have* ***an advocate*** *with the Father—Jesus Christ, the Righteous One* (First John 2:1 NIV). John is not encouraging us to sin, but it is an assumption that, as we grow in Christ Jesus, **we will sin.** The word **if**, in Greek grammar, assumes we all will sin. And when we sin, we have an advocate, Jesus, representing our case with the Father in the courts of heaven. Jesus is our **reconciliation.** He brings about the merciful removal of guilt and sin through divine **forgiveness.**

The Cross at Calvary is the key. It's our checkpoint where we must check ourselves daily for sin.

Did we repent from our heart?

Did we surrender our all to Jesus?

Did we die to the pleasures of our flesh?

CHAPTER 8

SAVED BY A SECRET WEAPON

Today you and I are in a spiritual battle with our enemy Satan. Each day that goes by may be our last.

Jesus is here, right now, as your extraction chopper ready to extract you up out of your sinful nature that your enemy, Satan, has you enslaved and addicted to. It may be drugs, alcohol, pornography, or meaningless sexual affairs. Perhaps you think your sins are so dark and sinful that you can't tell anyone. Whatever it is, *God loves you unconditionally—there is nothing that you have done that God hasn't already forgiven you for.* No matter what Satan has you addicted to or enslaved in, Jesus will **set you free,** and *when Jesus sets you free,* **you are free, indeed.**

Jesus knows your lost, desperate situation, and He has heard your hearts cry. He has just blown a hole through your thick, layered canopy of sin that you thought couldn't be penetrated and has dropped a rope ladder down to you.

Satan is telling you, "Wait! You need to clean yourself up first before Jesus will accept you!" But **your enemy is a liar**, a thief, and a murderer. He doesn't want you to know that Jesus loves you and has already defeated him and all his powers. Jesus wants you just the way you are—right now.

The very moment you hook into Jesus' rope ladder, every chain of bondage, addiction, and sin *will be broken and removed.* In its place, the Holy Spirit of God will come and fill you with the peace, joy, and purpose that can only be found in Jesus.

The rope ladder is swaying back and forth, waiting for you to decide to accept a new life with Jesus and hook up with Him, so that He can extract you up out of your sinful lifestyle and death-walk to Hell with Satan.

Jesus is knocking on your heart's door, saying, "Hook up with me. I'll save your soul and change your life. I'll give you purpose to live for, real peace, and joy.

All you have to do is just say this prayer with me out loud and mean it from your heart.

"Heavenly Father, in your Son's name, Jesus, I believe

and accept your plan of salvation for me. I believe that Jesus is the Son of God and my Savior. He died on the Cross at Calvary to save me, and I believe that your Holy Spirit raised Jesus from death, back to life, and that He lives today in heaven.

From the bottom of my heart, I am sorry for living my life in sin. I confess all the sins that I can remember and those that I cannot remember and ask you to forgive me. Wash me and cleanse me in Jesus blood. I love you, Father God. I want your will to be done in my life—your holy, righteous, and pure will.

Please send your Holy Spirit to come and live in me to sanctify and teach me all things. I desire this from my heart and mean every word. I give to you all I have to give. Whatever remaining life you allow me to live, I give to you. I want to please you! I want to have a relationship with you, Father. Thank you, Jesus, for saving me! You're my **Savior** and my **Secret Weapon**—you're my all in all.

You may be wondering: "Why do I need to speak this with my mouth out loud? Why couldn't I just think it?"

God knows everything about us—including the intentions of our heart. However, *Satan does not know our heart's intentions* and *is incapable of reading our mind.*

Satan needs to hear you say, "I want Jesus as my Master and Lord of my life."

In the spiritual realm, because we are Children of the Wicked One, the only way for God to take His rightful position as our Father—and for us become His Children—is, *"If you declare with your mouth, 'Jesus is Lord' and believe in your heart that God raised him from the dead, you will be saved. For it is with your heart that you believe and are justified, and it is with your mouth that you profess your faith and are saved. For, "Everyone who calls on the name of the Lord will be saved.'* Romans 10:9-10, and 13

God is willing and ready to forgive us, but we must declare with our mouth—out loud—our desire for God to become our spiritual father, instead of Satan.

When you say this prayer out loud, **Satan clearly hears you say,** "I believe in you, Jesus. I you love you and Father God, and all you have done for me. I want you to be my Savior!"

Satan hears you ask God to forgive you and accept you as His Child.

Satan heard you vow to live the rest of your life becoming a disciple of Jesus and doing the will of God.

Satan heard you ask God for His Holy Spirit to live in you and have His way in your life.

You just fired Satan. He no longer is your spiritual father.

He has no authority to come near you **unless** God allows it—**or** unless you speak with your mouth and say something that opens a spiritual door, allowing him and/or his forces permission to operate in or around you.

Now you know the true Gospel of Jesus Christ and how much God the Father loves you and desires for you to choose to accept Jesus and His plan of Salvation He has provided for you.

The choice is yours; however, you must choose while you're alive on Earth, because *there are no second chances in eternity.*

Are you ready to meet Jesus today? Maybe you thought you were saved and now you're not sure, or maybe you ran away from God like I did, in my teens.

Or maybe today is the first time you have been introduced to Jesus or fully understand who He really is and what He did for you.

Please understand that Jesus' defeat of Satan, his forces, and his works affects only those who *love, believe, and obey* Jesus' teachings and have been born of God's Holy Spirit.

If you don't believe in God's Only Begotten Son, Jesus, or if you say you believe but are living a lifestyle of sin, *then* you belong to Satan—the devil. He is your father.

If you think you can sit on the fence and remain neutral, indeed you can, but that territory belongs to Satan.

Uncommitted soldiers are referred by Jesus as "lukewarm" soldiers. God will have nothing to do with us if we are lukewarm. Jesus said, "I know your deeds, that you are neither cold nor hot. I wish you were either one or the other! So, because you are lukewarm—neither hot nor cold—I am about to spit you out of my mouth." (Revelations 3: 15-16)

Just trust in Him, and spend time listening and talking to Him. He is our commander, and we are His Rangers, preparing to capture prisoners of war for the Kingdom of Heaven.

There is **only one weapon** that can destroy Satan and his forces in your life, and that weapon is *the Word of God*.

Your Secret Weapon is **Jesus** and Jesus is, **"The Word of God."**

In the beginning was *the Word*, and *the Word* was with God, and *the Word* was God. Through him all things were made; without him nothing was made that has been made. In him was life, and that life was the light of all mankind.

The true light that gives light to everyone was coming into the world. *The Word* became flesh and made his dwelling among us. We have seen his glory, the glory of the one and only Begotten Son, who came from the Father, full of grace and truth. *He* came to that which was his own, but *His own* did not receive him. Yet to all who did receive *Him*, to those who believed *in His name*, He gave **the right to become children of God**—children born not of natural descent, or of human decision or a husband's will, but **born of God**. (John Chapter 1)

AUTHOR'S TESTIMONY

I AM AN EXAMPLE of the abundance of grace and mercy that God has extended and shown to those of us who were sinners and His enemies. But, because we have believed in Jesus and all that He is, we have become *Children of the Most High God.*

When I was young, I was raised in a strict, Bible-believing Church and made plans to be a Pastor and work for God, but I ended up running away from Him. I served another god—the god of pleasing myself and, later on in life, of pleasing the family that God blessed me with. Instead of putting God first in my life, I chased the definition of success defined by the companies I worked for. I put all the priorities of this world ahead of God.

At the age of 52, after spending most of my life pursuing prosperity, fame, earthly possessions, and pleasing my selfish desires, God finally broke me down enough that I would listen to Him.

I had just gone through a divorce, ending a 31-year marriage. My purpose for living life had vanished; I was a total failure to God, my family, and now my word. Everything I had lived for, I had failed to attain. I was broken spiritually and financially.

After 40 years of going in circles in the wilderness, I finally came to my senses and asked myself, "Is this the life my mother taught me to live? Is this the life I envisioned to serve for God? Is my life pleasing to God?" The answer was **no** to all the questions. It was obvious I had lived my life making decisions based on what **I wanted to do** and not involving God in any of my plans. I thought about coming back to God but wondered if He would even allow me to enter His kingdom after living a terrible, sinful lifestyle for 40 years.

So I began to search the Bible to see what God said about such a sinful person. I read that Jesus loved me so much that He came to Earth as God in the flesh and died for me, so that my sins would be forgiven if I confessed them to God. Jesus said that, no matter what sins I had committed, He would forgive me—stealing, lying, adultery, homosexuality, pornography, divorce, hating and mistreating people, and disobedience to His teachings and structures of creation. No matter what—all the sin I committed—God would forgive me as long as I turned from my wicked ways, repented, and sought to please Him.

Thirteen years ago, with a heart full of remorse, shame, and sorrow, I knelt down on my living room floor. I put my cigarette out and pushed my glass of scotch and water away. Without knowing how to pray, I prayed a little prayer. I asked God to forgive all my sins that I could remember and all those that I couldn't remember, and accept me just the way I was. I pleaded with God not to turn me away because I had been in the pig pen of life but to cleanse and wash me with the blood of Jesus, so that I would be clean to serve Him. I was willing to do anything, as long as he would allow me to become His son. I asked God for His Holy Spirit to come into me and give me the strength to live and do His will.

I began to tell God that I was not worthy to be a son in His kingdom, but before I could say anything else, I felt this big, strong, warm arm slide around me. I had never felt that kind of warmth before. The Holy Spirit of God was all over me. God accepted me before I could complete the sentence. I was free of sin—it was like riding on the warm feathers of an eagle's wing.

God said, "I have washed you and cleansed you in the blood of Jesus. I put clean clothes on you and have shod your feet. You are my son. **I am** with you. I have sealed you with the seal of the Holy Spirit, who will always be with you and will teach you all things.

"You must love me, obey me, and always walk in my ways. I'll never hurt you, and I'll never leave you. You will become a disciple and teach others the **Good News about me** and how to become disciples. I will be with you until the end of time."

The time has come to fall into a deep, loving relationship with Jesus. Remember what He told you: *"Behold, I am coming soon! My reward is with me, and I will give to everyone according to what he has done."* Revelations 22:12

Author,
Danny Clifford

If this book has blessed you, please tell others about it and consider giving this book as a gift to someone who is seeking to know the truth about God.

Contact us about buying these books at a discount to use as an evangelistic tool to win souls for Jesus. Our email is: **http://www.heartandsoulministriesinc.com**

You will enjoy Author Danny Clifford's other books:
Who Do People Say I Am?
Enter Through the Narrow Gate (Available Late Spring 2016)

God has anointed me as an Evangelist. As I go about teaching the "Good News Gospel of Jesus," the Holy Spirit will use me as He wills. What-ever gift the Holy Spirit needs, at the moment while I am ministering, He may use me or someone else to accomplish what God the Father wants done.

I am available, willing, and would love to come and share with you and your Church *the teachings* the Holy Spirit has *put in my heart to minister* to the *Church,* these **last days.**

Michelle, my beautiful wife and best friend, is anointed by the Holy Spirit of God with the gift of prophesy and the gift of a beautiful voice and spirit that brings a group of people—to a state of worshipping God. According to her work schedule, Michelle would love to come and fellowship with you. She loves to please and serve God.

email us at is:

http://www.heartandsoulministriesinc.com

May God bless you as you grow and do the Fathers Will.

Notes

Notes

NOTES